HARRY, RABBIT ON THE RUN

ADAM FROST

. . . would like you to know that he has
NEVER owned a pet rabbit.
The bunnies in this book are the product
of the author's wildly furry imagination.
Any resemblance to actual rabbits
(or hawks) living or dead
is entirely coincidental.

HENNING LÖHLEIN

. . . would like you to know that this
book has NOT been tested on any small,
cute creatures. No bunnies were harmed
during the drawing of the illustrations
for HARRY, RABBIT ON THE RUN.

Also by Adam Frost and illustrated by Henning Löhlein

RALPH THE MAGIC RABBIT

Praise for RALPH THE MAGIC RABBIT

'A brilliant comedy'
Sun

'I loved it. It is very exciting as well as funny'
Ryan, aged 8

HARRY, RABBIT ON THE RUN

Adam Frost

Illustrated by
Henning Löhlein

MACMILLAN CHILDREN'S BOOKS

First published 2007 by Macmillan Children's Books
a division of Macmillan Publishers Limited
20 New Wharf Road, London N1 9RR
Basingstoke and Oxford
www.panmacmillan.com

Associated companies throughout the world

ISBN: 978-0-330-44712-6

3 5 7 9 8 6 4 2

A CIP catalogue record for this book is available from
the British Library.

Typeset by Tony Fleetwood

Printed and bound in Great Britain by Mackays of Chatham plc, Kent

To my wife
A.F.

. . . and to mine.
H.L.

Meet the cast of
HARRY, RABBIT ON THE RUN

Harry

LIKES:
Exploring
Digging tunnels

DISLIKES:
Hungry hawks

Gus

LIKES:
Eating carrots
Eating apples
Eating in general
Sleeping

DISLIKES:
Heights
Caves
Being eaten

Humphrey

DISLIKES:
Being mistaken
   for a rabbit
Riff-raff
Gus

LIKES:
Being a hare

Russell

LIKES:
Glenda
Singing songs
  about Glenda
Daydreaming
  about Glenda

DISLIKES:
Upsetting Glenda
Being away from
  Glenda
Frank the
  Handsome
  Rabbit

Glenda

LIKES:
Russell
Daffodils

DISLIKES:
Her nose
Beetroot
Not knowing
  where
  Russell is

Shane

LIKES:
Dangerous
  experiments
Using long words
Coming to the
  rescue

DISLIKES:
Peace and quiet

Chapter One

Harry the Rabbit was having a good day. He had just managed to eat ten carrots in five minutes, which was a personal record. Before that, he had found a great big hollowed-out log, which he spent ages running around in, sticking his pink nose out of one end and then the other. And earlier on, he had come across a giant haystack in the middle of a field, which was great for bouncing on, sliding down and hiding radishes inside.

Now he was on the way to his best

friend's rabbit-hole, bounding down a grassy bank, while bees droned and butterflies fluttered around him. As he stopped to nibble a dock leaf, he felt a rush of air behind him. A hawk swooped, picked him up by the scruff of the neck and carried him off into the sky. Harry saw branches, then the tops of trees, and then clouds, and then he passed out.

When he came round, he couldn't see anything – just mist. He looked down and could only just make out his feet, dangling helplessly in mid-air. He looked up and was able to see the hawk's yellow legs and white stomach, but the mist hid everything else. As it got windier and mistier, he noticed icicles clinging to his fur. He was about to pass out again, when the wind dropped, the mist cleared, and there in front of him was a huge mountain with a shaggy-looking nest balancing on top of the highest peak. The hawk circled the mountain, dropped Harry into the nest and flew away. Harry lay there in the nest, playing dead till he was sure the hawk had really gone.

'Well, *this* has definitely spoilt my day,' Harry said to himself as he stared up at the sky. He was thinking about what he should do next, when a trembling voice began to echo in his ears:

I long to go home to my hole in the ground.
I wish I was back in my burrow.
Instead I'm scared stiff at the top of a cliff
And I'll probably get eaten tomorrow.

He sat up and saw a small brown rabbit on the other side of the nest. The rabbit was staring into space and singing quietly. He began another song:

> Will I ever see my friends again
> Hopping through the misty glen?
> Where the mud is warm and gooey
> And the grass is long and chewy.
> The puddles can be stepped and leapt in.
> The ditches can be crept and slept in.

'So how come you're up here too?' Harry said.

The other rabbit snapped out of his trance. 'Oh, hello,' he said vaguely.

'Were you brought here by the hawk?' Harry asked.

'Oh yes,' the other rabbit said with a nervous laugh. 'I'm just sitting here, waiting for him to tuck in.'

'He'll definitely eat us then?' Harry said.

'Well, why do you think he's brought us here?' the other rabbit replied. 'To show us the view?'

Harry pondered this for a second. 'So why hasn't he eaten us already?' he said.

'Because hawks don't feed, they *feast*,' the other rabbit said. 'They always have at least three courses. I'm the starter, you're the main course and he's gone to find his pudding now.'

Harry jumped up. 'Crikey! We've got to get out of here!'

He ran across the nest and peered out over the edge.

'That's just what I was thinking,' the other rabbit said blankly. 'I mean, I would

have left earlier, but I didn't want to hurt his feelings.'

Harry grew dizzy as he stared down at the huge drop and the clouds, hundreds of feet below. He sat back down in the nest with a sigh. 'Maybe we should try calling for help,' he said.

'I've been doing that all morning,' the other rabbit said sadly, 'but I'm happy to give it another go.'

They both took a deep breath –

'HELP!' they shouted.

'HELP!' they shouted again.

For a few seconds, there was nothing. Then they heard their voices echoing in the distance. HELP HELP HELP HELP HELP HELP.

'Blast! This is pointless. Nobody's going to hear us,' Harry said.

'I know, but I quite enjoy the shouting. HELP! HELP!' the other rabbit cried.

Harry was leaning over the edge again.

He leaned so far over that the nest began to tilt to one side.

'W-w-watch out,' the other rabbit said, 'you'll kill us both.' He took two steps backwards to counterbalance Harry and make the nest steady again.

'I'm not staying here just to get eaten,' Harry said. 'I'm going to jump.'

'You're going to w-what?' the other rabbit stammered.

'I'm going to jump,' Harry said. 'Down there.'

'But you'll break your neck.'

'Yes, but at least that hawk won't get to eat me.'

'But maybe – maybe – he won't come back,' the other rabbit said. 'He might get lost or – or – injure his wing.'

'Then we're still stuck here, aren't we?' Harry said. 'Look, there is no other way out of this.' He stood on the edge of the

nest and crouched down, like a swimmer preparing to dive.

'But what about me?' the other rabbit said. 'You can't leave me here.'

'Then come with me,' Harry said.

'No, no, you stay here,' said the other rabbit. 'Look, I'll show you my great new dance. Watch this. And this.' He swayed from side to side and waved his arms in the air.

'Look, mate – what's your name, by the way?' Harry asked.

'Gus the Bunny,' said the other rabbit.

'I'm Harry the Rabbit,' said Harry. 'As soon as that hawk comes back with his third course, we're finished. You said so yourself. So come on, give me your hand. We'll both jump at the same time.'

'N-no, honestly,' Gus stammered.

'We don't have much time. Come on, take my hand,' Harry said.

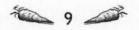

'It-it's such a long way down,' said Gus.

'Trust me, we'll be OK,' said Harry.

Gus closed his eyes and held out a trembling paw.

Chapter Two

Down they fell, hurtling through the air, Harry scowling and Gus howling, with their fur blown back and their ears fluttering in the wind.

After thirty seconds of falling, Harry noticed they were about to hit the side of the mountain.

'ROLL UP INTO A BALL,' he shouted.

'WHAT?' Gus hollered.

'ROLL UP INTO A BALL,' Harry shouted again.

'THROW UP INTO A SHAWL?' Gus yelled.

'NO. ROLL UP INTO—'

But then there was a thud and a crunch, they bounced once, bounced twice, slithered down a slope and came to rest on a narrow ridge overlooking another sheer drop.

Gus was the first to clamber to his feet He patted his ears and squeezed his tail. 'I'm alive. Hooray! HOORAY!' he exclaimed.

Harry stood up slowly. 'Ow,' he said as he stretched his back legs. 'Ooh,' he said as he tried to turn his head.

'Well, things are certainly looking up,' said Gus. 'It's funny, I had a feeling your plan would work. I know I looked frightened on the outside, but I was calm on the inside.'

Harry limped to the edge of the ridge and looked down.

'In fact, I was about to suggest a similar plan myself,' Gus continued. 'I was just waiting for the right moment to bring it up. I'm good at plans. Back home, I'm known as

"The Best Planner in the Manor".'

'In that case,' replied Harry gruffly, 'could *you* work out how we're going to get down from this ledge?'

This seemed to startle Gus. He slowly took in his surroundings, edging gradually backwards till he was flat against the mountainside.

'Oh no, we're still g-going to die, aren't we?' Gus stammered. 'That hawk's going to fly down and find us. Or else we'll starve to death. Or, you know, what if we *roll over in our sleep*.'

Harry tested the edge of the ridge with his paw; it crumbled away and fell into the valley below.

'Oh well, what's the problem? We can just jump again,' continued Gus with a mad laugh. 'We can keep jumping. What are we waiting for?'

'No, wait!' exclaimed Harry. 'Up there!'

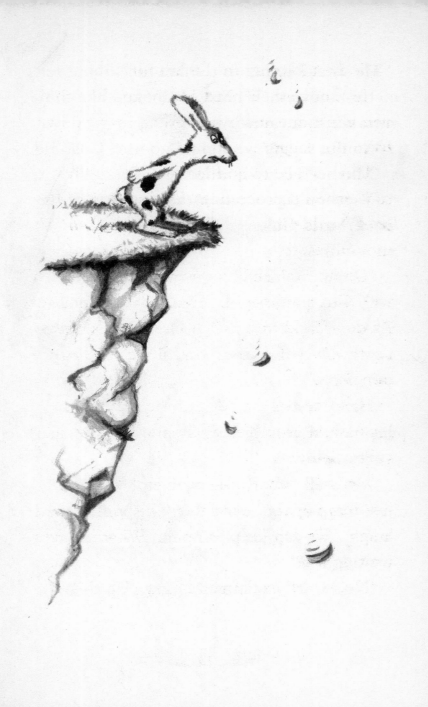

He was pointing to a small hole about ten metres above their heads. It looked like the entrance to a cave or burrow.

'You're saying we should go up?' Gus said.

'Maybe.' Harry nodded.

'We should proceed *in the direction of the hawk*?' said Gus.

'Look, there could be shelter up there,' Harry said, 'or *food*.'

'Oh, there'll be food all right. Us,' Gus said.

'Well, let me know if you come up with a better idea,' said Harry, and he turned round and started to climb. The mountainside went straight up, like a tree trunk.

Gus spluttered and whimpered for a while and then said, 'It's too steep. We'll never make it.'

Harry was already a metre up. He looked over his shoulder and said, 'This is our best option. When that hawk finds out we've escaped, he'll start looking for us. We need to be out of sight.'

'I won't be out of sight,' said Gus. 'I'll be halfway up that slope, hanging on for dear life.'

'Look, just copy me,' said Harry. 'Use the cracks in the rock to pull yourself up. If you get stuck, just shout, and I'll come down and help you.'

Gus cautiously put his paw into the first crack – it seemed to be full of green slime.

This is even worse than the last plan, he thought. 'Wait for me!' he said.

The two rabbits made slow progress. After a few minutes, Harry got tired and laid his head against the mountain. Gus was a metre behind, his fur covered in dust and dirt.

Just then, a herd of five or six mountain goats bounded past them. They didn't seem to notice that the mountain went straight up; they trotted by like they were crossing a field or a heath.

A short while later, a young-looking goat stopped next to Harry and said, 'Excuse me, did a herd of mountain goats pass you just now?'

Harry was running out of breath, but managed to say, 'Yes.'

'Which way did they go?' the goat asked.

'Up,' Harry panted. 'Up.'

The goat paused for a moment and looked down at Harry.

'I say, are you all right down there?' he asked.

Harry nodded and swallowed.

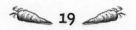

'It's just, you seem to be clinging on. Rather than bounding along. I know it takes a bit more effort, but bounding along really is the way to go.'

Harry clung on tightly as a gust of wind swept over the mountain.

'Well, I'd better go,' the goat said. 'My parents get annoyed when I wander off.' He sniffed the air and dashed away.

Harry and Gus kept climbing.

The sun went down and they were still several metres from the hole in the mountainside.

'I'm tired, hungry and cold, and now I can't see what I'm doing,' said Gus.

'Yes, well, I'm not exactly jumping for joy either,' said Harry.

Then the first drops of rain fell on their fur.

'Oh no! Now we're going to get wet as well,' said Gus.

And it will make the rocks more slippery, Harry thought.

The two rabbits battled on as it got darker and wetter. The rain made Harry look sleek, while Gus turned into a wiry furball.

'This is more than any rabbit can stand,' muttered Gus.

Finally they reached the hole in the mountainside. They lay down in the entrance and didn't speak or move for ten minutes.

'Come on,' Harry said finally. 'We'd better move further inside.'

Gus shook his head.

'I don't care any more. I'm ready to be eaten. I'm just going to lie here till he comes.'

'Gus, don't be ridiculous,' said Harry. 'Come inside.'

'I give up, I surrender,' said Gus. 'Mr Hawk! Dinner's ready! It's your favourite! Fresh rabbit!'

'Gus, he WILL hear you,' Harry hissed.

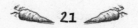 21

Gus started to sing:

I'm tastier than a hedgehog
And juicier than a shrew.
You could try me in a pie
Or use me in a stew.

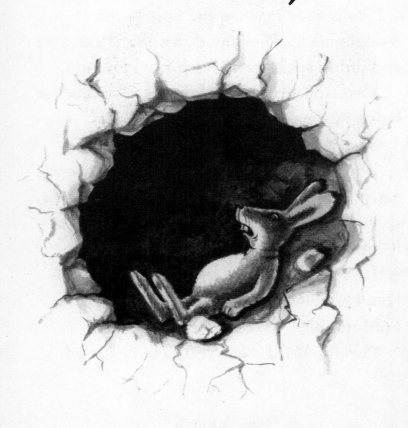

Then their ears stuck straight up. They heard a fluttering, then a flapping, and then a swooping sound. Even though it was pitch black, they knew that only one creature made noises like that. The hawk was closing in on them.

They dived inside the cave and peered out into the night – four big round eyes blinking in the darkness.

'Do you think he heard us?' Gus whispered.

'You were *singing* – of course he heard us,' Harry whispered back.

A gust of wind rushed into the cave as an outstretched wing brushed the rocks above them. Harry grabbed Gus's arm and pulled him further back into the cave. A feather from the hawk's tail floated towards them and landed at their feet.

'He'll keep circling till we come out,' Harry said, 'so we're going to find out where this cave leads.'

They felt their way forward, placing one paw on the cave wall and using the other to reach out into the darkness. Gus thought about the hawk waiting outside and then he thought about the monster that probably lived *inside* the cave. He didn't know whether to run away or stand absolutely still.

The two rabbits moved slowly onward, banging their heads on rocks, stumbling into

boulders and falling over on top of each other.

'This is ridiculous,' Harry said. 'We need more light.'

'If only we had some carrots,' Gus said, 'then we'd be able to see in the dark. Can't we stop now?' he pleaded. 'We must be a safe distance from the hawk.'

Harry thought about this. It had been an incredibly long day.

'OK, let's get some sleep,' he said.

'Hooray!' Gus exclaimed. 'Sleep! I love sleep! Especially deep sleep. Though, that said, I like naps too.'

Harry lay down against the cave wall and Gus settled down next to him.

'I slept for three days once,' Gus continued. 'Sometimes I sleep on my back like this, and sometimes I roll up into a ball. Oh, sleep is just great!'

Harry closed his eyes and let his mind drift: he was galloping up the rock face like a mountain goat. Just as he dropped off, he felt his arm being tugged.

'Harry,' said Gus.

'What?' said Harry.

'I can't sleep,' said Gus.

'What?' said Harry.

'It's the ceiling,' said Gus, 'it's *moving*.'

'Moving?' Harry said. He opened his eyes and stared up at the roof of the cave. He

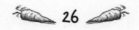

vaguely made out a jagged black outline, rising and sinking.

'They must be bats,' he said.

'B-bats?' Gus said.

'They wake up about now,' said Harry. 'Hold on to me and I'll hold on to you.'

'Oh no,' said Gus. 'This is officially the worst day of my life. Worse than my fourth birthday party, when nobody came.'

A bat dropped from the roof, whisked past their ears and fluttered towards the cave entrance.

'It's worse than when my tail was struck by lightning and I went bald for two weeks,' continued Gus.

Another bat slipped down from the roof and flitted past them, and then another.

'Yes, this is definitely the worst,' said Gus as they were buffeted by another four or five bats.

Then every bat in the cave started to

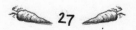

squeak, which became a squeal, which became a shriek, which turned into an ear-piercing, blood-curdling scream. Harry and Gus were knocked over backwards as hundreds of bats poured over them and burst out of the mountainside.

When it was all over, Harry and Gus lay there, staring at the cave wall in a daze. Finally they fell asleep.

At dawn they were woken up when all the bats rushed back into the cave.

'Arghh!' screamed Gus.

'Not again!' shouted Harry.

The bats landed one by one, hanging upside down by their claws, until the whole roof was black again.

Gus turned to Harry and said, 'I think that was probably the worst *night* of my life too.'

'At least it's daytime. We can see where we are now,' Harry said.

Light was streaming into the cave, not just from the entrance, but from an assortment of cracks and holes in the rock.

'Come on, Gus, we'll soon be home,' said Harry.

Chapter Three

Harry headed further into the cave. Gus plodded after him, singing softly to himself:

> I'd rather be pelted by turnips
> Or swept out to sea by a wave.
> I'd rather have spears
> Lodged in my ears
> Than stay with you here in this cave.

When Gus was singing the song through for the fourth time, Harry exclaimed angrily,

'Look, I'm not forcing you to follow me. You can go wherever you want!'

Gus fell silent again.

'If it wasn't for you, I'd probably have got off this mountain by now,' Harry said.

Gus stared at his feet for a few minutes. 'Sorry,' he said.

As they got further into the cave, the roof got higher and the walls grew cooler. Stalactites went drip drip drip, forming shallow pools on the ground. Harry had to admit, as they turned another corner, that

the cave didn't seem to lead anywhere.

Suddenly a low groaning noise echoed around the cave. It was followed by an eerie gurgle and a sinister hiss that chilled Harry to the bone.

'Sorry,' Gus said, 'that was my stomach.'

Harry breathed a sigh of relief. 'OK, I'm hungry too. Maybe we should turn back.'

There was another low rumble, followed by a loud crack.

'Crikey, you are hungry,' said Harry.

'It-it wasn't my stomach that time,' stammered Gus, looking up and around in terror.

Dust and grit fell from the cave roof.

'Get down!' Harry shouted and threw himself on top of Gus.

A sheet of rock slid down behind them with an almighty crash. They were swept further into the cave and buried underneath a mound of rubble. A few minutes passed and then Harry and Gus emerged, coughing and spluttering and brushing dust off their fur.

Harry looked at the wall of rock that now stopped them going back the way they had come.

'That was a pretty big cave-in,' he muttered. 'We're lucky to be alive.'

'Lucky!' Gus said. 'Did you say lucky? Did you call ME lucky? I'm sorry, I thought lucky was if an apple fell off a tree and rolled down into your burrow, or if you were born with the strength of fifty rabbits and could jump over trees. I didn't think it meant *being crushed by falling rocks.*'

Harry started walking further into the cave.

'Where are you going now?' asked Gus.

'Well, this is the only way we *can* go,' Harry said.

'Oh good,' said Gus, scrambling after Harry, 'let's hope our lucky streak continues.

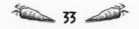 33

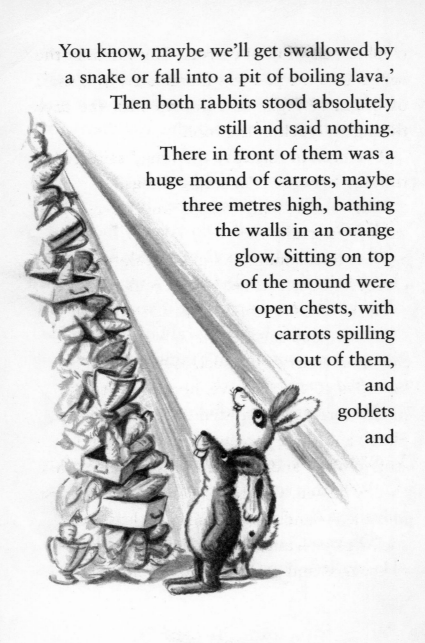

You know, maybe we'll get swallowed by
a snake or fall into a pit of boiling lava.'
Then both rabbits stood absolutely
still and said nothing.
There in front of them was a
huge mound of carrots, maybe
three metres high, bathing
the walls in an orange
glow. Sitting on top
of the mound were
open chests, with
carrots spilling
out of them,
and
goblets
and

trophies, also full of carrots. The carrot at the very top of the pile was illuminated by a shaft of bright sunlight that poured into the cave through a crack in the roof.

'I've been in this cave too long,' said Gus, rubbing his eyes. 'I'm seeing things.'

'You're not seeing things,' said Harry. 'The carrots are really there.'

Next to the mound, a giant sculpture of a carrot had been carved out of rock.

Harry and Gus looked at each other. Gus's stomach started to rumble again and, this time, Harry's stomach joined in. They bounded across the cave, hopped on to the pile of carrots and started eating frantically. Harry had three carrots in each paw and stuffed more and more into his mouth till his cheeks bulged. Gus had disappeared headfirst into the mound till only his hind legs were sticking out – and they jerked around as he rummaged and grabbed and swallowed.

After a few minutes, both rabbits were about
halfway up the mound, with carrot juice
down their fronts and all over their faces.

'Rr wrdr rr orr,' said Harry.

'Wr wr?' replied Gus.

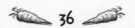

'I wonder who this belongs to,' said Harry, swallowing a mouthful of carrot.

'Who cares?' said Gus.

The cave was silent again, except for the crunch of carrots being bitten in half and the thunk of dislodged carrots hitting the ground.

'I say, old chap,' Gus said, 'would you care for a carrot?'

'You know, I'd like that a lot,' Harry replied. 'Thank you kindly.'

Gus passed Harry a carrot, which Harry ate. A few moments later, Harry bit the end off another carrot.

'You must try this one,' Harry insisted. 'It has just the faintest hint of apricots.'

Gus grasped the carrot and took a bite.

'Mmm, this reminds me of a carrot I found in a ditch last spring when I was hiding from an owl just outside Chipping Ongar,' Gus said.

Harry smiled.

After eating five more carrots each, both rabbits began to feel sleepy. They yawned and stretched and made themselves comfortable on the carrot mound.

They were soon jolted awake by a booming voice.

'WHO DARES TO EAT THE SACRED CARROTS OF KING MUNGO?'

The voice seemed to come from everywhere and nowhere. It echoed around the cave.

Harry and Gus looked at each other.

'WHO FAILS TO RESPECT THE MOST ORANGE AND POINTY OF VEGETABLES?' the voice continued.

'I thought this was too good to be true,' said Gus.

'A CURSE SHALL FALL UPON ANYONE WHO DINES IN THIS SHRINE,' the voice thundered.

'Let's get out of here,' Harry said.

 38

'I'm right behind you,' Gus said.

But the two rabbits were so full of food they could hardly move. They puffed their way down the side of the mound, while the voice continued to boom, 'YOUR FATE IS SEALED.'

By the time they reached the bottom of the mound they were exhausted.

'What's going to happen to us?' Gus wondered aloud, panting heavily.

'Something unpleasant, would be my guess,' Harry replied, looking around and trying to work out where the voice was coming from. 'Look, I'm sorry, Gus,' he went on. 'I really thought we stood a chance. I really believed we could make it back home.'

'Hang on a minute,' Gus said, and wandered over to a boulder at the side of the cave.

'LEAVE THIS PLACE,' the voice echoed.

'There's a duck down here with a
megaphone,' said Gus.

'What?' Harry said.

He stood beside Gus and looked behind
the boulder.

There was a duck holding a megaphone
made out of a hollowed-out carrot.

'Are you responsible for the scary voice?'
Harry said.

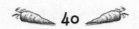

The duck looked from side to side and then nodded.

'What's the big idea?' Gus asked.

'I'm the keeper of King Mungo's carrots,' said the duck.

'Are you serious?' Gus said.

'Who's King Mungo?' Harry asked.

'I'm not sure,' replied the duck. 'But I know he was really keen on carrots.' He pointed at a message carved into the wall behind him:

DITCH THE RADISH.
SHUN THE CHIVE.
FORGET THE LETTUCE.
LET CARROTS THRIVE.

So how come you're here?' Gus asked.

'Family tradition,' said the duck. 'My grandfather was the first Keeper of the Royal Carrots, then my father, and now me.'

'Oh,' said Gus.

There was a brief moment of silence.

'So what are you going to do to us?' Harry asked.

The duck sighed. 'Well, obviously you weren't supposed to see me,' he said.

'OK,' said Harry.

'Most animals have normally run away by this point,' the duck continued.

'Well, we *nearly* did,' said Gus helpfully.

'But essentially I'm supposed to visit King Mungo's curse upon you and your sons unto the seventh generation,' said the duck.

'And what does that involve?' Gus asked.

'Well, *mainly* it involves throwing carrots at you,' said the duck.

'Oh, OK,' said Gus.

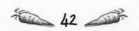

There was another awkward pause.

'Look,' Harry began, 'how about we just take a couple of carrots for the road and pretend this whole thing never happened?'

The duck looked unsure. 'You can take one carrot each,' he decided.

Harry looked at Gus. Gus shrugged.

'OK, it's a deal,' said Harry, 'provided you tell us how to get out of this cave.'

'Oh, that's no problem,' the duck said. 'See that hole in the rock? Crawl through it, turn right and head for the light at the end of the tunnel.'

'Great,' Harry said.

Just before he crawled inside the hole, Gus turned to the duck and said, 'You could come with us if you wanted to.'

But the duck had gone back behind his boulder.

Chapter Four

Harry and Gus hopped through the tunnel. When they reached the other end, they found themselves on a steep and narrow track which zigzagged down the other side of the mountain.

'Ah, fresh air!' Gus exclaimed.

Harry looked up warily. 'Let's hope that hawk doesn't fly round this way.'

'Oh, you leave him to me,' said Gus. 'Now I've eaten all those carrots, I can take anything on. Mountain lion. Grizzly bear. Puff adder.'

He let out a scream and leapt behind Harry. 'What's that? What's that?'

A puffy white blob was sitting on the path in front of them.

'It's a cloud of some kind,' said Harry. 'That's funny, I didn't think we were that high up.'

'What are we going to do?' asked Gus, looking over Harry's shoulder.

'We can just walk through it,' said Harry. 'Stay close behind me.'

Harry walked up to the cloud and disappeared inside. Gus took two steps forward and then hesitated.

'Are you sure about this?' Gus asked.

'Yes,' said Harry, from inside the cloud.

'This is going to work?' said Gus.

'It'll be fine,' said Harry, inside the cloud.

Gus stepped inside the cloud. There was a white blur and then they were standing on the other side. Their fur

was covered in a thin film of water.

'Yuck, I'm all tense now,' said Gus. 'I need some food to cheer me up.'

'Food?!' Harry exclaimed and started walking again. 'But you just ate about fifty carrots.'

'I know,' said Gus. 'But that was almost half an hour ago.'

'What about your carrot "for the road",' said Harry. 'Did you take one?'

'Yes, but I ate that in the tunnel back there,' said Gus.

'Well, you know,' mumbled Harry, 'I suppose you could have mine.' He pulled a carrot out of his fur and held it out.'

'Oh no, Harry, I couldn't,' said Gus.

'Go on, go on, take it,' said Harry, half closing his eyes.

'No, look, just – just give me half,' said Gus.

'OK,' Harry said with a nod. He snapped the carrot in half and gave Gus a chunk.

'But you've got the bigger half!' protested Gus.

Harry sighed and gave Gus the bigger half, which Gus gulped down immediately.

As they carried on walking, Gus started to chatter. 'You know, it's a shame we couldn't have stayed in that cave. It was full of food and there were no hawks to distress us.'

'Yes, but it's not like being at home, is it?'

Harry replied. 'You know, I keep thinking about the fields outside my burrow. They're not particularly beautiful and there's not really that much to do. In the evening, they're usually full of gnats. But home is home. Nowhere else feels the same.'

Harry turned round, but Gus was no longer beside him. He looked back up the path and saw Gus standing on a narrow ledge, staring at a branch that stuck out from the side of the mountain. At the end of the branch, there was a single apple.

Harry walked towards Gus and said, 'Come on, we haven't got time for this.'

'Look at it, just look at it, it's . . . perfect,' murmured Gus.

Harry replied, 'Gus, you just ate half a carrot. We've got to keep going.'

'I haven't eaten an apple for over a week,' said Gus.

'You can't be serious!' exclaimed Harry. 'We are still being chased by a hawk, you know.'

He tugged Gus's arm, but Gus was rooted to the spot.

'If only I could reach it,' said Gus, 'but I can't work out how.'

'All right,' said Harry with a growl. 'If I crawl out there and get you your apple, will you promise never to ask for food again, never to wander off, but to follow me *in total silence* till we get to the bottom of the mountain?'

'Oh, I promise, I promise!' Gus exclaimed, clapping his paws with excitement.

Harry lay down flat on his stomach and started to crawl along the branch. It was

long and thin, and it started to creak as Harry got closer to the tip, where the apple was hanging. He glanced down quickly and shuddered – the ground was a very long way away.

As he reached out to grab the apple, the branch suddenly bent right round and he almost fell off the end. He looked over his shoulder and saw Gus, hanging on behind him.

'Have you got it yet?' Gus asked.

The branch snapped and the two rabbits tumbled through the air, hurtling past rocks and stones, past another flock of mountain goats, past ridges and ledges and past several confused-looking birds, who swerved to avoid them.

As they continued to fall, Harry manoeuvred himself next to Gus and started to strangle him.

'You – idiot – both – killed,' grunted Harry.

Gus managed to push Harry away. 'Look, I was hungry, OK?' Gus shouted. 'It's not something I can control.'

Harry tried to grab Gus again, but Gus had spun further away.

'I've had just about enough of you!' shouted Harry.

'And I've had enough of you too,' replied Gus. 'Always having a go at me.'

'Fine,' Harry said. 'From now on, we split up.'

'Yes,' said Gus, looking down, 'into about a hundred pieces.'

They were about to start fighting again, when they landed with a crunch on a bundle of sticks.

For a few moments, they both lay on their backs, looking up at the sky.

'We've survived – again,' murmured Gus.

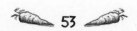

'It seems so,' said Harry. The apple hit him on the nose and bounced off. 'Ow,' he said. 'Look, Gus, I'm still really annoyed with you.'

'But why?' Gus replied. 'We're alive – and we're even further down the mountain.'

They sat up and their faces froze. They were in the middle of a large nest, being stared at by a small brown rabbit and a big grey hare.

'Hello, I'm Humphrey,' said the hare, 'and this is Russell.

Did that *dreadful* hawk carry you off too?'

'Oh n-no,' stammered Gus. 'This is t-t-
terrible.'

'Of all the rotten luck,' mumbled Harry.

'Well, there's no need to be rude,' sniffed
Humphrey. 'A simple "Good afternoon"
would be nice.'

'There's no escape,' whimpered Gus.
'There are too many nests, too many hawks.'

Harry was leaning over the edge of
the nest, looking down the mountainside.
Although they were on a lower peak this
time, it was still a very long way down.

'Don't shout at me, Harry,' pleaded Gus.
'I'm already buckling under the strain.'

'I'm not going to shout at you, Gus,'
insisted Harry, 'but we've got to get out of
here. Now.'

'Look, I don't know what you two are
talking about,' Humphrey said, 'but Russell
and I are halfway through a wonderful game

of I Spy. You're very welcome to join in.'

'Humphrey, Russell,' Harry said, 'my friend and I are jumping out of this nest. Unless you want to get eaten, I suggest you come with us.'

'Jumping?' said Humphrey. 'But that's madness. Besides, Russell hasn't guessed my "something beginning with n" yet.'

'Suit yourself,' said Harry, 'but when the hawk comes back with his next course, you'll be sorry.'

Russell began to wail, 'Glenda, Glenda. Tender, slender Glenda.'

'Who's Glenda?' asked Gus.

'*Who's Glenda?*' protested Russell. 'The most beautiful bunny in the world. Her eyes are as green as a cucumber, her nose is as pink as a radish.'

'Sounds like the hawk should be eating her, not you,' said Gus. 'But listen: I know my friend sounds mad, but I'm afraid he's right. Jumping is the only way out.'

'No, no,' replied Russell, 'I'm going to stay here and think about Glenda. You know, Glenda and I had a "happy song" that we'd sing whenever things got on top of us. I can sing it now if you like.'

Before Gus could answer, Russell starting singing:

Imagine a carrot as big as a house,
So tall it has snow on the top.
I'd slowly begin
To eat my way in,
Then get to the middle and stop.

And then the next day I'd invite
    friends to stay
And we'd throw lots of parties and balls.
In the orangey light
We'd dance through the night
And (now and then) nibble the walls.

We'd chomp and we'd swallow till the
    carrot was hollow,
Then slowly fall into a slumber.
And the very next day
We'd all go out to play
And find a gigantic cucumber!

Gus was about to say how much he liked
Russell's song, when a rush of cold air swept
over the nest. The four rabbits turned round
and saw the hawk hovering right in front of
them with a terrified baby rabbit dangling
from its claws.

'Jump, Gus, jump!'
shouted Harry.
Gus ran over and
took Harry's paw.
'Come on, you
two!' Harry shouted at
Humphrey and Russell.
Russell stammered, 'I-I should stay
and fight the hawk. Then Glenda
would l-love me even more.'

'She'll think you're an idiot,' said Harry.
'Come on. You too, Humphrey.'

The hawk squawked and swept down
towards them.

'This is all most troublesome,' said
Humphrey. 'But look, if you leave me and the
hawk alone for a few minutes, I'm sure I can
sort this whole thing out.'

'We've got to go NOW!' exclaimed Harry.

'He is a mere *bird*, after all,' Humphrey
continued. 'Like a blue tit or a sparrow.'

Gus grabbed Humphrey by the arm and said, 'You're coming with us. End of story.'

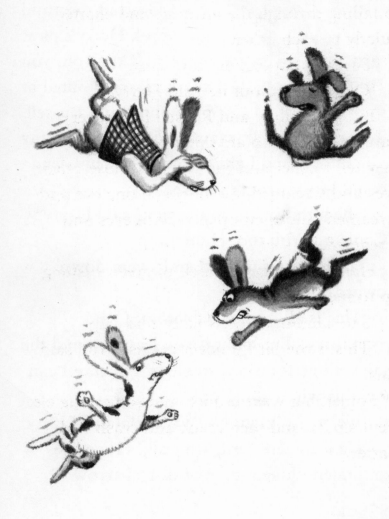

The four rabbits jumped as the hawk landed in the nest. Harry and Gus were used to falling through the air now, and chatted quietly to each other.

'Sorry about earlier,' said Gus.

'Oh, forget about it,' said Harry.

But Humphrey and Russell had never jumped off or into anything before, so, as they fell further and further, they closed their eyes and screamed, then opened one eye and screamed, and then opened both eyes and screamed.

Harry saw a large block of green rushing up to meet them.

'Safe landing, Gus,' Harry said.

'This is the bit I'll never get used to,' said Gus.

Something went crunch and something else went smash and then crack and crash and clatter.

Chapter Five

Harry was the first rabbit to come round. For a few moments, all he could see was the sky and a few clouds. Then he felt the branch underneath him and sat up. Slowly he realized he was sitting at the top of a tall pine tree, looking out over a large forest. He glanced sideways and saw Gus sitting in the tree next to him. Then he saw Russell in the tree in front of him. He looked around for Humphrey, but couldn't see him anywhere.

'Is everyone OK?' Harry shouted.

'I th-think so,' Gus replied groggily,
rubbing his nose.

'I don't believe it!' Russell shouted from
his treetop. 'I'm alive!'

Then Humphrey's voice came from a tree
that was some distance away.

'I wouldn't say OK,' the voice said. 'I'm stuck
up a tree. I've snagged one of my ears on a
branch. And my bottom is full of pine needles.'

'Look, let's rest for five minutes,' Harry

shouted. 'Then we start climbing down!'

'Climbing? I'm sorry, but I couldn't, I just couldn't,' Humphrey's voice replied. 'In fact, I demand to be taken back to the nest. I wish to forget this whole episode.'

'It's all right up here, isn't it?' Gus said from his treetop. 'You can see for miles. I think I'd really enjoy living in a tree.'

'What? Instead of a rabbit-hole?' Harry asked.

'Oh no, I'd still have a burrow,' Gus said. 'The tree would be my *second* home. For weekends and holidays, you know.'

'But surely the birds and squirrels would get annoyed,' Harry said, 'if the trees were full of rabbits.'

'Oh, there'd be room for everyone,' Gus said. 'Birds, rabbits, pigs. A row of ponies. All adjusting to a new life in the trees.'

'But wouldn't – hang on – what's that noise?' Harry said.

The ground was being pounded by something very heavy. Then that stopped and one of the trees started to shake very violently. The trunk creaked and the branches trembled. Then the pounding began again.

Harry peered down through the pine needles and pine cones and saw a big brown shape lumbering around on the forest floor.

'Crikey, it must be a bear,' he whispered to himself.

'W-what's going on?' Russell asked.

'Listen, everyone. I think there's a bear down there,' Harry shouted. 'He must have smelt us. He's going to shake these trees to try to get us down. So hold on tight.'

'Oh no,' Gus whimpered.

'If I don't survive,' Russell called out, 'tell Glenda that I love her. And not to forget me and marry Frank the Handsome Rabbit.'

Harry's tree was the first to be shaken.
Harry hugged the tree-trunk and clenched his
teeth. The forest became a green blur as the
bear pushed and shoved. Pine needles went
everywhere as branches clattered against each
other and snapped.

Russell's tree was next. Harry and Gus
watched anxiously as Russell lost his grip and

slid along the branch he was sitting on. The bear shook and shook, and Russell hung on to the end of the branch with one paw, using the other to fend off falling twigs and pine cones.

The bear stopped and moved on to Gus's tree. Gus clung on bravely as the roots creaked and the tree almost toppled over. When the bear stopped, Gus was hanging upside down from a broken branch, covered in a blanket of pine needles, knobbly sticks, dust and insects.

Finally a tree in the distance started shaking and they heard Humphrey's voice protesting.

'Stop that, you brute! Some animals have no manners. You won't get away with this, you know. I have friends in very high places.'

'Who does he know in high places?' Russell asked Harry.

'The hawk maybe? Or a mountain goat?' Harry replied.

The bear started to get bored and ambled off into the undergrowth.

'I think he's gone,' Harry said. 'Let's wait for a bit and then climb down.'

'D-down?' replied Gus. 'Harry, are you sure?'

'In situations like this, I often ask myself, "What would Glenda do?"' Russell said. 'And I feel pretty sure that, in this situation, she'd say *stay away from the bear*.'

'Yes, but if we stay up here too long, the hawk will see us,' Harry said, 'and the bear's already moving away. Look.'

They watched the trees around them being shaken, and then the trees in the distance, and then the trees on the far horizon.

'OK, let's get going,' Harry cried.

Gus and Russell looked at each other across the treetops. They sighed and started to climb down.

'Humphrey,' Harry called out, 'we're going.'

'I'm staying here,' came back Humphrey's voice. 'I need time to recover. I've been treated disgracefully.'

'Fine,' said Harry gruffly and continued to climb down.

Ten minutes passed and the rabbits were still stuck in the treetops. The branches were so spiky and tangled that it was difficult to find a way through.

'Listen,' Harry called out, 'in between my tree and Russell's tree there's a big patch of mud. Let's jump down and try to land in it.'

Gus looked down at the forest floor.

'I'll miss it, Harry,' he said. 'I'll land on something hard instead.'

'I'm pretty sure Glenda would be against it,' Russell said from the top of his tree.

'Well, Glenda's not here, is she?' Harry answered angrily.

'All right, don't rub it in,' said Russell, holding back a sob.

'Look, it'll be fine. Aim for the middle.
And land feet first,' said Harry.

Gus and Russell looked across at Harry
and nodded slowly.

'Humphrey, we're going to jump!' Harry
called out.

'You go ahead,' Humphrey's voice replied.
'I wish to be alone with my thoughts. Please
don't disturb me again.'

'Get eaten then, see if I care,' muttered
Harry. He ran as fast as he could along the
branch he was on, then bounced off the end.

Russell looked at Gus and asked, 'Is he
always like this?'

'He's usually worse,' Gus replied. He
closed his eyes and ran off the end of his
branch.

Russell tried to work out what Glenda
would say and got so confused that he fell
off his branch and tumbled down behind
Harry and Gus.

Harry landed with a splat. Gus landed
with a squelch. Russell landed with a squish.
Mud went everywhere. Harry sat up and
mud flew off his arms and landed on Gus.
Gus wiped his mud off and got more mud
over Russell. Russell tried to wipe all the
mud off his fur but his paws were so muddy
that he ended up wiping more mud in.

'At least we're all OK,' Harry said.

'I've been better,' said Gus. 'This stuff just won't come off.'

Just as they had all finally brushed and washed the last traces of mud out of their coats, Humphrey landed next to them and covered them with mud all over again.

'Oh no!' they all exclaimed.

'That's charming, that is,' Humphrey replied. 'I decide to join you; I realize you'll

be lost without my wisdom and courage, and this is all the thanks I get.'

Humphrey had managed to avoid getting a single speck of mud on his coat – it had all gone everywhere else.

'Still, I suppose we've all had a long day, so I forgive you,' said Humphrey. 'We'll say no more about it.'

Russell, Harry and Gus started to brush the mud out of their coats again.

Humphrey took a step backwards. 'Be careful,' he said. 'Some mud nearly went on me then. Now, I wish to forget the jumping and the tree and the bear and the shaking and everything else. So let's play a game. Twenty questions? Hide and seek?'

'We've got to keep moving,' Harry said, pulling mud out of his ears. 'The hawk might see us. The bear might see us. And it'll be dark soon.'

'I'm not moving again today,' Humphrey

insisted. 'Perhaps not even this week.'

'Look, there's a woodland path over there. Let's follow that and see where it leads,' Harry said.

He pointed at a narrow track that wound in and out of the trees.

Gus looked unsure. 'It might lead somewhere awful,' he said.

'It might lead home,' Harry replied.

'I think I've forgotten where home is,' Gus said, 'and what it looks like.'

'Come on, Gus, it won't be much further,' said Harry. 'You can't give up on me now.'

Chapter Six

Harry and Gus made their way through the forest to the winding track. Russell hesitated and then ran to catch up with them. Humphrey watched the three of them moving through the trees.

'On your heads be it,' he sniffed. 'I try to help, but I'm clearly just wasting my time.'

Then he heard something scuffling in the undergrowth and nearly jumped out of his skin. As he raced towards Harry, Russell and Gus, he said to himself, 'After all, I can't just *abandon* them, can I? What if something happened to them? How could I live with myself?'

The path took the four rabbits deeper into the wood. Harry and Gus were walking side by side, followed by Russell, who occasionally stopped to pick flowers for Glenda. Twenty metres behind them, Humphrey strolled along with his nose in the air, grumbling about the 'shabby trees' and the 'tatty shrubs' and the fact that everything was covered in moss and fungus.

An hour passed. The path got narrower and then wider, it got steeper and then flatter, it curved to the left and turned to the right. But it only led to more pine trees, stretching away on all sides.

Suddenly the earth started to shake and the sky began to rumble.

'Oh no,' said Russell, 'thunder and lightning.'

'It's OK,' said Harry. 'It's only Gus's stomach. You'll get used to it.'

'Sorry,' said Gus. 'I'm getting hungry, that's all.'

'Once we're out of this forest,' said Harry, 'we'll look for food, I promise.'

'But that could be *days*,' complained Gus. He put his fingers in his ears as his stomach started to gurgle and hiss.

Harry looked at the path as it slipped behind a row of trees. He wondered if they were going in circles.

'Look, Harry, look!' Gus cried out. He pointed at a large carrot that was sitting next to the track. Behind it, there was another carrot. A trail of carrots led off the path and into the darkness beyond. They seemed to flicker like candlelight; they seemed to sparkle like jewels.

'Cool,' said Gus. He picked up the first carrot and swallowed it whole.

'Hang on, Gus, wait –' stammered Harry.

'Here you are, Russell . . . Humphrey,'

said Gus. He picked up the next two carrots
and tossed them at Humphrey and Russell.

'Thanks,' said Russell.

'Can you *pass* it to me next time?'
Humphrey said.

'Come on, Harry,' said Gus, 'it'll be like
King Mungo's cave.'

He tore off into the woods, following
the trail of carrots, eating some, picking up
others, leaving the rest for Russell, Humphrey
and Harry.

'Gus, we should stay on the path!' Harry
called out.

But Gus was weaving in and out of the
trees, getting smaller all the time.

Harry breathed a deep sigh. 'Come on,' he said to the others.

They followed the trail of stray carrots that Gus had left behind. The trees got closer and closer together and the ground became bumpier and rockier. Harry kept looking over his shoulder because he didn't want to lose sight of the path, but it was no good, it had gone: there was no turning back.

When they caught up with Gus, he was on the edge of a small clearing of dried-out grass. Gus was carrying a huge pile of carrots, holding them in place with his chin. Chewed-up carrot was spilling out of his mouth.

'This is – mm – mm – amazing,' he said. 'Who do you think left them here?'

The trail led across the clearing, with the carrots getting bigger and juicier all the time.

'Gus, I really don't like the look of this,' Harry said.

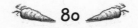

'Absolutely,' said Humphrey. 'You'll give yourself indigestion.'

'What do you mean – mm – mm?!' exclaimed Gus. 'This is every rabbit's dream.'

He waddled across the clearing, tucking more carrots under his chin.

The other three rabbits tried to stay on his tail, occasionally pausing to eat the odd carrot themselves. They passed through another dense patch of woodland, before reaching another clearing.

'Hey, everyone!' Gus called out. 'It looks like they run out here.'

The trail of carrots led into the middle of the clearing, and then stopped.

Gus followed the trail, continuing to pick up carrots, dropping two for every one he grabbed.

Harry, Humphrey and Russell had reached the edge of the clearing.

'Gus, no, I've got a bad feeling about this,' Harry said.

Gus was standing in the middle of the clearing, holding the last carrot.

'What do you mean?' he asked, biting the carrot in two. Then the ground underneath him gave way and he disappeared.

'Where did he go?' Russell asked.

'Gus!' Harry exclaimed and ran to the middle of the clearing.

Harry could see that someone or

something had dug a deep pit and laid
branches and leaves over the top of it. Gus
was stuck in the bottom of the pit, looking up
at Harry with big frightened eyes.

'Why do you keep doing things like this?!'
Harry exclaimed.

Humphrey and Russell joined him at the
edge of the pit.

'Oh well, can't be helped,' Humphrey said.
'We'd better keep going.'

'What are you talking about? We're not
leaving him there,' Harry said.

'Harry, I know you were fond of the
strange little creature,' said
Humphrey, 'We all were. But you've
got to think of the future now.'
Then something gave them a big
shove, and they all tumbled forward
into the pit and ended up in a big
furry heap at the bottom.

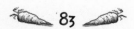

When they came to, they were tied to a stake, surrounded by firewood. A bear ambled over with an armful of sticks and branches. He dropped his bundle at the rabbits' feet and then headed back into the woods. He sang as he went:

When eating rabbits for your tea
Always cook them thoroughly.
Eat them slowly – never fast –
And always save the ears till last.

For a few moments, the rabbits were too
dazed to work out what was going on. It was
Gus who first realized what was happening.
'Harry, are you awake?' he whispered.

'The bear's going to eat us.'

Gus was on one side of the stake, Harry was to his left, Humphrey was to his right and Russell was behind him, tied to the other side of the stake.

The other three rabbits were jerked awake by Gus's words. They immediately tried to wriggle free, but they were tied too tightly to the stake with vines and knotted grass.

The bear reappeared with another bundle of sticks. He added them to the pile of firewood, then lumbered back into the trees, whistling happily.

'Well, this has all turned out rather well,' Humphrey said.

'There must be a way out,' Harry said, struggling again.

'Don't worry,' Russell murmured, 'Glenda will save us.'

'What did you say?' Harry asked.

'Glenda will save us,' Russell said, and his

eyes went all misty. 'I've been gone for two days now. She'll wonder where I am and she'll come looking.'

'And do what?' Harry growled. 'Wrestle the bear to the ground? Poke him in the eye with a carrot? Stop going on about stupid Glenda.'

'How dare you?!' Russell huffed. 'Come here and say that.'

'How?!' exclaimed Harry. He struggled and tried to edge round to Russell's side of the stake.

Russell snarled and puffed and tried to edge round towards Harry.

The bear returned, dropped another load of firewood and went back into the forest. The rabbits were now waist-deep in branches.

'Leave Harry alone; it's not his fault,' Gus cried out, and he tried to edge round towards Russell.

'That's true, it's your fault, you furry little

cretin,' Humphrey said, and tried to shuffle round towards Gus.

'Don't you touch Gus!' Harry said, and edged back towards Humphrey.

All four rabbits were struggling, but none of them could move more than a few millimetres.

'*Psst!*' went something behind a tree.

The four rabbits continued to hiss and snap at each other. '*Psst!*' went the noise again. The four rabbits stopped. They saw, leaning out from behind a tree, a rabbit wearing glasses and holding a big stick. His face was covered with mud and he was camouflaged with leaves and branches.

'Is the coast clear?' he whispered.

The four rabbits looked up and around. Then they all nodded.

'OK,' the rabbit with the glasses whispered.

He scuttled across to the pile of firewood and started gnawing the vines that were tying the four rabbits to the stake.

Harry got free first. He joined in and helped the rabbit with the glasses nibble through the remaining vines.

When everyone was free, they scurried off into the woods, in the opposite direction from the one the bear had taken.

'Who *are* you?' Russell asked.

'Shane the Brainy Bunny,' said the rabbit with the glasses. 'Pleased to meet you.'

Chapter Seven

Shane led the other rabbits to the edge of the forest. The trees stopped and a narrow path wound down the rest of the mountain.

'Wow, we're nearly at the bottom!' declared Harry.

'Judging from the amount of calcium in the rocks and the high levels of moisture in the air, I'd say we're five hundred metres up. That's two days' walk,' said Shane.

The rabbits hopped over towards a boulder and lay down behind it. The day was coming to an end and they needed to rest.

'How did you get here?' Harry asked Shane as they all huddled together.

'I was in the field outside my burrow,' Shane replied, 'and I was very excited because I had just spotted a variety of hyacinth that usually only grows in Outer Mongolia. As I was running home with the news, a hawk picked me up and swept me off into the sky. It was a good job I was carrying this.'

Shane held up the stick he had been carrying.

'Why?' asked Harry.

'Because
this is no
ordinary
stick,' said
Shane. 'Look
at how sharp
the top end
is. When the

hawk was flying over these woods, I stabbed him in the belly, and he dropped me. Not long afterwards, I found you.'

'That happened to us too,' said Russell. 'We were kidnapped by hawks.'

'We're all lucky to be alive,' said Harry.

'Especially with him around,' said Humphrey, pointing at Gus.

'All right, stop that,' warned Harry. Then he added, 'Thanks for rescuing us, Shane.' And everyone else thanked Shane too.

Then they all closed their eyes and tried not to think about hawks, bears or falling down mountains.

That night, Harry had a series of bad dreams. He kept seeing the face of the baby rabbit that they had left in the nest when he, Gus, Russell and Humphrey had escaped from the hawk. He was running through a rabbit warren, and every time he turned a corner, the baby rabbit was standing there in the middle of the tunnel. He was in the forest, playing Hide and Seek with his friends, and every time he found a place to hide, the baby rabbit was there already, smiling at him strangely.

Harry woke up with a start. His whole body felt cold and stiff. Then he looked down and saw that a thin layer of snow had settled on his fur. Gus was curled up next to him, singing softly:

I've never been this cold before.
My feet are frozen to the floor
And I can hardly move my jaw
Or feel my fingers any more.
I do not think they'll ever thaw.

Humphrey was half awake, rubbing his eyes and yawning. Next to him, there was an empty space where Russell and Shane the Brainy Bunny had been. They had left two rabbit-shaped outlines in the snow, with grass poking through.

Harry stood up and looked around. Snow had covered everything so that, where there had previously been peaks and ridges on the mountain and colour and movement everywhere – with the trees swaying and rivers gushing, now everything was smooth and still and silent.

Harry turned to the left and saw Russell making a rabbit out of snow. He had just

used a pine cone to make its tail.

As Harry approached, Russell turned and spoke.

'It's meant to be Glenda,' he said. 'Glenda and I first met in the snow.'

Harry nodded. 'Sorry I had a go at you earlier,' he said, 'when we were tied up.'

'That's OK,' said Russell. 'I know it's annoying, but I can't stop thinking about Glenda.'

'Maybe you should try thinking about something else,' said Harry. 'You're only torturing yourself.'

'Like what?' Russell asked.

'I don't know, like daffodils,' said Harry.

'They're Glenda's favourite flower,' said Russell.

'All right, chestnuts then,' said Harry.

'Glenda lives next to a horse-chestnut tree,' said Russell, 'and her fur is a kind of chestnut brown. And nuts are her second favourite food, after carrots.'

Humphrey and Gus joined Harry and Russell.

'So where's Shane?' Harry asked.

Humphrey and Gus shrugged.

'He wasn't around when I woke up,' said Russell.

Harry looked back up the mountain. He noticed a trail of rabbit paw prints leading away from where they had slept towards an uprooted tree. Harry followed the paw prints and the other rabbits followed Harry.

The trail zigzagged across a frozen pond and ended at a cluster of luminous blue mushrooms.

'Wow, look at what Shane found,' Gus said. 'Do you think you can eat them?'

'Oh no,' Harry murmured, 'oh no oh no oh no.'

He pointed at a grey feather in the snow.

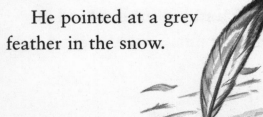

'Look,' he said.

There were talon tracks next to the paw prints.

'Please no,' Harry said.

He picked up Shane's glasses. A few metres away, Shane's pointy stick was poking out of the snow.

The four rabbits stared at each other, then up at the sky, then back at each other.

They dashed towards a patch of ferns and dived inside.

'Do you think it's still out there?' whispered Russell.

'Do you think it can see where we're hiding?' whispered Gus.

'Who do you think it'll go for first?' said Russell. 'Humphrey? He's the biggest.'

'Maybe there's more than one,' murmured Gus. 'Maybe there are four hawks. One for each of us.'

Water dripped around them as the snow on the ferns slowly melted.

'It's very unfair,' sniffed Humphrey. 'Shane seemed like such a clever and distinguished rabbit.'

'I know,' said Russell, 'I know.'

'Why didn't the hawk take one of you three?' lamented Humphrey.

A gust of wind blew through the ferns, showering the rabbits in snow crystals.

Harry was staring

intently at the ground, grinding his teeth and clenching his paws. Gus was fidgeting next to him, but he didn't notice.

Harry closed his eyes and muttered to himself.

Finally he said, 'We have to go and rescue Shane.'

Gus and Russell both said, 'What?' at the same time.

'We have to go and get Shane back,' said Harry.

'Get him BACK?' said Russell.

'He saved our lives,' said Harry. 'If it wasn't for him, we'd all be dead meat.'

'Don't be silly, Harry,' said Gus. 'If you go after him, you'll be even deader. You'll get eaten. Or starve to death. Or freeze to death. Or slide off the mountain. Or get buried alive in an avalanche.'

'Look, I'm not saying this is going to be fun,' said Harry. 'I'd much rather forget Shane and go home. But he needs our help.'

Harry stuck his head out of the ferns, looked up at the sky and stepped out into the cold air.

'Snow madness,' said Humphrey. 'Same thing happened to my second cousin. Nothing you can do.'

Gus stuck his head out of the ferns, but went no further.

'Harry,' he hissed, 'the hawk will get you. You'll end up as rabbit burgers or rabbit cutlets or RABBIT RASHERS.'

Harry kept walking.

'Look, you can all stay here if you want,' he said, 'but I'm going back up the mountain.'

Harry stood up on his hind legs and sniffed the air. Gus hopped nervously towards him.

Then a shadow swept across the snow. A hawk swooped, grabbed Gus by the shoulders and took off.

'Gus!' yelled Harry.

Harry ran as fast as he could, jumped as high as he could, and grabbed hold of Gus's ankles.

'Harry! Gus!' exclaimed Russell.

Russell bounded out of the ferns, leapt into the air and clung on to Harry's legs. This jerked the hawk downwards. But it flapped its wings harder and faster and started rising again.

'What on earth are you all doing?' huffed Humphrey. 'You can't just leave me here.'

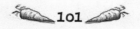

101

He jogged across the snow, flung himself into the air and threw his arms around Russell's knees.

The four rabbits hung there in a chain underneath the hawk. The hawk's wings were beating, but it wasn't getting any higher: it was stuck in mid-air, wobbling and wavering. It seemed to make one last effort, twisting into the wind; then it dropped the rabbits and vanished.

There were four soft thuds as the rabbits landed in the snow. Harry was the first to stand up. 'Did you see what happened there?' he said excitedly. 'Did you see what happened?'

'I nearly got eaten,' said Gus quietly.

'It couldn't take off,' Harry went on. 'The four of us together were too heavy! Don't you see what this means? We can go and save Shane now, no problem.'

Russell was getting to his feet. 'It *was* pretty amazing.'

'Russell,' said Harry, 'think what a story you'll have to tell Glenda when this is over.'

Russell nodded. 'You're right, Harry. I'll come with you.'

'Oh Harry,' whimpered Gus, 'why are all your plans so scary and dangerous?'

'But the hawks can't hurt us any more,' said Harry.

'What about the bears?' said Gus. 'And the bats and the snakes and the wolves and the foxes?'

'We'll steer clear of the woods this time,' said Harry.

'Well, it sounds like you three have got it all sorted out,' said Humphrey. 'How about I keep going down the mountain and, when I get home, I'll tell everyone about your plight

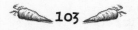

and we'll all come and rescue you. For a small fee, of course.'

'But the four of us have to stick together,' said Russell. 'That's how it works.'

'Then why don't you all come with me?' Humphrey asked. 'We'll be home by teatime. You can all come to mine and meet my Aunt Tabitha.'

Gus looked undecided, but Harry put his hand on Gus's shoulder.

'Let's go,' said Harry.

Harry hopped towards the nearest slope, followed by a sniffling Gus and a sombre-looking Russell.

'Why don't they listen to me?' growled Humphrey, trooping after them, 'I'm a born leader of rabbits. I have a natural air of authority.'

The four rabbits climbed towards a narrow ridge.

Harry suggested that they march along in

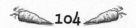

single file. He was in front, holding a sharp
stick, Gus and Humphrey were in the middle,
looking out for hawks, and Russell was
behind them, also armed with a stick.

Harry sang to himself as he climbed:

We're the rabbit army,
Heroic and aloof.
Our paws are deadly weapons,
Our fur is bullet-proof.

If you're a hawk or owl or stork
You'd better change your habits.
With might and skill, we'll fight until
The world is safe for rabbits.

Gus nudged Harry and tried to speak but nothing came out. Finally he whispered, 'Hawk!'

Harry looked up and said, 'OK, hold on to each other. Now!'

The four rabbits quickly huddled together and put their arms round each other's shoulders.

'Is it too late to r-run away?' murmured Gus.

The hawk plummeted and dug its talons into Russell's shoulders. It tried to take off, but Russell clung on to Humphrey and Harry. The hawk flapped its wings twice, lifted Russell a few centimetres from the ground, squawked in frustration and flew away.

'Keep holding on to each other!' shouted Harry. 'It's not over!'

The hawk was a dot in the sky, circling higher. Then it dropped down again.

This time it grabbed Harry, who held on tightly to Russell and Gus. The hawk flapped its wings harder than ever, yanking Harry upwards with all its might. All four of the rabbits felt the ground drop away. A second later the hawk was gone; they were sitting side by side in the snow.

'I knew it, I knew it!' Harry exclaimed, jumping up and clapping loudly.

Russell rubbed his shoulder and smiled to himself.

'I must admit, that was quite satisfying,' Humphrey said.

'I'm sorry,' Gus said, 'but that was still incredibly stressful.'

'I know, Gus,' said Harry, 'but it won't happen many more times. We'll find Shane soon, I know it. We'll be home in a day or two. Everything's going to be different from now on.'

They started to walk up the mountain

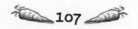

again. Twice Gus and Humphrey spotted a
hawk and they all huddled together. But both
times the hawk hovered above them for a few
seconds, then turned away.

It began to snow again in the afternoon.
By early evening, they were caught in a
blizzard.

'OK, let's dig,' said Harry.

'Dig?' said Humphrey. 'I'm sorry, I don't dig.'

'Fine,' said Harry, 'then stay outside.'

Humphrey folded his arms and muttered
something about not being a mole or a water
rat or an earthworm.

Russell, Gus and Harry started to dig a
tunnel in the snow. Within half an hour, they
were sitting in a cosy snow-burrow, fairly
warm and very tired.

Harry wondered if he should call
Humphrey inside, but fell asleep a split
second later.

The next morning Harry was the first to emerge from the tunnel. The sun was warm and the air was crisp. He saw Humphrey, still in a sulk, with his arms folded, frozen in the middle of a block of ice.

'Oh no!' Harry exclaimed.

He ran over to the ice block and started thumping it with his paws and gnawing at it with his teeth.

The noise woke up Russell and Gus and they poked their heads out of the tunnel.

'Oh no!' they both said.

Then they looked at each other and started laughing. Harry stopped whacking the ice and started laughing too. Finally, Gus said, 'We should probably get him out now.'

'Yes, I expect it's cold in there,' said Harry.

'No, not because of that,' Gus said. 'It's just – if a hawk comes by, there need to be four of us or we'll get caught, right?'

Harry nodded and the three rabbits chopped and chomped away at the ice until Humphrey was able to wriggle free.

'Are you OK?' Russell asked.

Humphrey said nothing.

'Do you want to come into the burrow and warm up a bit?' Gus asked.

Humphrey didn't reply.

Harry, Russell and Gus looked at each other and began giggling all over again.

Then Harry and Gus
noticed that Russell had
stopped laughing.
'Look,' he said,
'a nest.' He
narrowed his
eyes. 'With two
rabbits in.'
Right in front of
them, balanced on
a narrow ledge,
was a hawk's nest with
four ears sticking out of it.

'Can you see who it is?' Harry asked.

'No,' said Russell. 'We need to get closer.'

The rabbits looked up at the sky and
checked for hawks. Then they began to climb
towards the nest.

Halfway up, they found a crack in the
rock face and stopped for a rest.

Humphrey sighed and said, 'I suppose I

should thank you for getting me out of that block of ice.'

Harry, Russell and Gus looked at each other in surprise.

Humphrey went on, 'Then again, I suppose I've kept you all alive so far. So I guess that makes us even.'

The rabbits rested for a little while longer, then began to climb again.

Soon they could make out the bottom of the nest, balancing on one corner of the ridge.

'Hello!' the four rabbits shouted.

Two faces appeared over the edge of the nest.

'Oh, hello there!' Shane called out.

'Shane!' Gus and Russell exclaimed.

'Shane, are you OK?' Harry cried out.

'Oh yes,' said Shane, 'quite all right, thank you. Touch of frostbite, that's all.'

The other rabbit in the nest leaned further out and her big pink eyes opened wide.

'Russell!' she cried.

Russell blinked in surprise.

'Glenda!' he shouted.

He began to quiver with excitement. 'It's Glenda! I don't believe it!'

He started to sing:

Oh Glenda, my precious, my angel.
No one else matters to me.

Glenda sang back:

Oh Russell, my sweetheart, my darling.
You're all that a rabbit should be.

Harry, Russell, Gus and Humphrey scrambled the last few metres, climbed over the steep ridge, and jumped into the nest.

'Glenda, what are you doing here?' Russell asked, unable to believe his eyes.

'I thought I'd try to rescue you,' Glenda said. 'Silly really, I know. I'd only gone about a hundred metres when a hawk got me. Still, everything's all right now, isn't it?'

Russell and Glenda hugged each other and danced around.

Harry and Gus hugged Shane; Humphrey shook Shane's paw.

'Have you made new friends, Russell?' Glenda asked.

So Russell introduced Glenda to everyone and told her about their adventures on the mountain.

'Oh, you're all so brave!' Glenda exclaimed.

They all blushed and fidgeted and looked

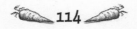

at their feet, even Humphrey.

'Now, I'm rather glad you're all here,' Shane said, 'because it gives me a chance to test my theory. I think that the combined weight of five rabbits and one hare will be just enough to bounce the nest off the top of this ridge. If we jump up and down at the same time.'

'He was telling me about this before,' Glenda said. 'It's all very clever.'

'You see, once the nest hits the mountain, it will act as a kind of sledge or toboggan, reaching speeds of around fifty or sixty miles per hour.'

'Hang on – hang on,' said Gus.

'So all we have to do is boing up and down like this,' said Shane, pogo-ing on the spot.

'But won't we fall out?' Gus blurted out. 'And if we don't, won't we die when the nest hits the mountain?'

'No, no,' said Shane, still jumping,
'there's a less than forty-per-cent chance of
serious injury.'

'Forty per cent! Isn't that a lot?' Gus
asked.

'Hardly anything,' Harry chipped in.
'Come on, Gus. Let's boing.'

The rabbits all started to jump and
the nest started to creak. The ridge
cracked and rumbled, the nest tilted
sideways and the rabbits felt the ground
give way.

'Aaaaarrrgh!' screamed Russell,
Humphrey, Harry, Gus and Glenda.

'Fascinating,' said Shane.

The nest landed with a jolt and started
sliding along in the snow.

'OK, lean back,' said Shane.

They all leaned back and the nest moved
faster.

'Lean to the left,' said Shane.

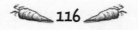

They all leaned to the left and avoided a large grey boulder.

'And hold tight,' said Shane as they hit a large mound of snow and flew twenty metres through the air.

Soon the rabbits got the hang of it, and slalomed around trees, slithered along frozen rivers and ducked under low branches and tangled shrubbery.

Then they heard a gentle rumble behind them.

'Hmm,' said Shane, looking over his shoulder, 'There was always a twenty-one-per-cent chance that this would happen.'

A few minutes earlier they had dislodged a stone from the mountainside. This had rolled along behind them, gathering snow as it picked up speed, till now it was a gigantic snowball, twice the size of a haystack, bouncing and thundering behind them and getting closer by the second.

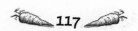 117

'Oh no,' said Gus. 'I knew this was too good to be true.'

'We'll be fine if we head for that yawning crevasse,' said Shane. He pointed straight ahead. The ground ran out and a huge canyon split the mountain in two.

'Are you sure?' Harry asked, looking at the snowball, then the canyon, then back again.

'Quite sure,' said Shane, 'just lean back and hold on to the sides of the nest.'

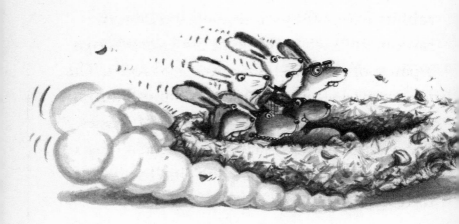

The rabbits headed straight for the canyon, hit the edge just as the snowball caught up with them, and took off high into the sky. Harry, Gus and the others all stared straight ahead while Shane looked over the edge at the gaping black hole beneath them.

Harry lost track of how long they were in the air. Were they rising or falling? Were they even the right way up? He couldn't think or speak. He couldn't even breathe.

Then with a bump the nest landed on the other side of the canyon. It spun round and round, spiralling faster and faster till the rabbits were sick with dizziness. The snow ran out abruptly and the nest skidded across a patch of mud and hit a tangle of roots. The rabbits were flung out of the nest and into the air. They flew past a pond, a field of daisies and a dried-out ditch before landing in a heap of leaves, rolling over twice and finally coming to rest halfway down a small green hill.

'Look, Russell, home!'
said Glenda. She stood up
and pointed at a row of
trees in the valley
below.
Harry
also got
to his
feet. He
recognized
a meadow full
of red poppies. His
rabbit-hole was just
behind it!
'Food!' exclaimed
Gus. He leapt up and hopped towards a
blackberry bush. He used both paws to pick
the juicy berries, stuffing them into his
mouth as fast as he could, not caring when
half of them fell out again as soon as he
started chewing.

'Gus!' said Shane. 'Watch out!'

Shane was looking up at the sky. Harry and the others also looked up.

Two hawks had dropped out of the clouds.

'It's OK,' Harry said. 'They can't hurt Gus, as long as we go with him.'

'What do you mean?' Shane asked.

So Harry quickly explained how four rabbits were too heavy for one hawk.

'Of course!' exclaimed Shane. 'That makes perfect sense! They can't lift more than half their body-weight. Oh, I must see this in action!'

Shane waved his paws in the air.

'Mr Hawk! Over here!' he shouted.

Harry jumped on top of him and wrestled him to the ground.

'We'll show you tomorrow, OK?' Harry said. 'It's been a long day.'

Then they all joined Gus and ate blackberries till they were full.

* * *

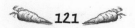

121

From that day forward, the world was a much better place for rabbits. Harry, Gus, Humphrey, Russell, Glenda and Shane the Brainy Bunny told every rabbit they knew how the hawks could be beaten.

Of course, Harry and his new friends also decided that it would be much safer all round if *they* stuck together too. So Humphrey, Shane, Harry and Gus spent a week with Russell and Glenda. Then Glenda, Russell, Humphrey, Shane and Gus came to stay in Harry's rabbit-hole. When they all visited Shane, Glenda brought along two of her friends, Cheryl and Beryl.

Cheryl fell in love with Harry, and Beryl fell in love with Gus, which was awkward, because Harry had fallen in love with Beryl, and Gus had fallen in love with Cheryl. But then Cheryl decided she preferred Gus after all, and Beryl decided that Harry was actually quite sweet, and everybody was happy, except for Humphrey, who didn't understand why both Cheryl and Beryl hadn't fallen in love with him.

Sometimes the rabbits talked about their time on the mountain. They all agreed that it had been brilliant in spite of the danger and the stress.

Russell said that they should have another holiday together, maybe somewhere warm this time, like how about the seaside? But Gus said that the problem with the seaside was the sea, and the problem with the sea was the sea monsters, with their long tentacles and sharp teeth and huge claws. Then Harry told Gus not to worry because they had beaten the hawks after all and that sea monsters would be a pushover.

The eight friends did everything and went everywhere together. You'd often see them in a long line, hopping through the fields or scurrying through the woods. Shane would usually be at the back, holding his latest invention – a rope ladder for climbing down into holes, a long stick for spearing apples in trees or a catapult for flinging pebbles at hawks. He told all the animals in the forest that he was also working on a 'hoverpack', an ingenious invention that would allow rabbits to fly higher than hawks. Everyone thought that Shane was crazy, although a young mouse called Eloise once swore she saw Shane with a wooden propeller strapped to his back, hovering five metres above his friends. But everyone else in the forest said that this was impossible, that Eloise was seeing things, and that no rabbit in the world could ever be that brainy . . .

. . . Could he?

THE
END

Read another utterly nutty story from Adam Frost and Henning Löhlein . . .

Do YOU want to be different?

Then visit

Ralph the Magic Rabbit! With one simple wish he will make your wildest dreams come true . . .

Sid the snail sets off on a life-changing adventure - only to discover the secret to true happiness lies a little closer to home.

An extract from . . .

RALPH
THE
MAGIC
RABBIT

'I think I should pay that mad-scientist snail a visit,' Sid said to himself.

It took him half an hour to get there, during which time he noticed a trail of bright green smoke pouring from the entrance to the tree-trunk. As Sid got closer, he couldn't help noticing that it smelt of Stilton cheese.

Sid put his head inside the tree. 'Hello?' he said. There was no reply.

'Hello?' he said again.

Sid took a deep breath and slid inside.

Through the smoke, Sid made out a snail with a white moustache, sitting behind a table built from tree-bark. The snail had a mouse's skeleton hanging up next to him, and lumps of chalk on a ledge above his head. A pile of dazed ants lay on the table in front of him.

'Ah, another guinea pig,' said the scientist.

Sid looked confused. 'I always thought I was a snail.'

'Just sign here, here and here,' said the scientist. Like most snails, he had two pairs of feelers. His eyes were on the end of his long pair, and he used his short pair like hands to move things around. He gave Sid a form with his short feelers. Sid read:

I, the undersigned, allow Professor Snail Q. Snail to singe, pummel, perforate, bury and shred me in the name of science.

Sid replied quickly, 'Look, I've only come here because I want to go faster.'

'Faster? Oh, I see,' said the mad scientist. 'I'm so sorry. My mistake.' He told Sid to sit down on a pile of dock-leaves.

'I need your help,' said Sid. 'I was wondering if you had some kind of potion to make me speedier.'

The mad scientist gave his feelers a twirl. 'I suppose I could cook up some martlet and grebe juice.'

'And will that make me go faster?' asked Sid.

'No, it will make your head and your tail change places,' said the mad scientist.

'Hmm. I was sort of more interested in something to make me faster,' said Sid.

'In that case,' said the mad scientist, 'you could try some Tungo Powder.' He lifted up an acorn-cup full of yellow powder from under the table.

'And will that increase my speed?' asked Sid.

'No. Rub three grains on to your forehead and you'll turn into a King Edward potato. Watch.' He picked up an ant from the table and demonstrated.

'Impressive,' said Sid when it was over, 'but I'm still really taken with the "speed" idea.'

'Well, how about a Thunderclap Hat?' the mad scientist asked. He produced a cap made of a broken eggshell and two sprigs of heather.

'And what will that do?' asked Sid.

'Try it on and see,' said the mad scientist.

'No, no, just tell me,' said Sid.

'Your shell will burst into flames.'

'Look,' snapped Sid, 'I don't want to catch fire, or grow wings, or anything like that. I just want to be the fastest animal ever.'

'OK, OK,' said the scientist, giving a deep sigh. 'I'm afraid it can't be done. Scientifically speaking, snails are like dribble or sweat. They trickle. They ooze. Ask the Three Wise Snails if you don't believe me.'

Ralph the Magic Rabbit
Is a truly splendid creature.
His supernatural powers
Are his most attractive feature.

He can make you big and strong
And wise and clever too.
With one click of his fingers
He'll make your dreams come true.

But Ralph does have one tiny flaw
That limits his appeal.
He may have powers unlike ours,
But is this rabbit REAL?

A selected list of titles available from Macmillan Children's Books

The prices shown below are correct at the time of going to press. However, Macmillan Publishers reserves the right to show new retail prices on covers, which may differ from those previously advertised.

All Pan Macmillan titles can be ordered from our website, www.panmacmillan.com, or from your local bookshop and are also available by post from:

Bookpost, PO Box 29, Douglas, Isle of Man IM99 1BQ
Credit cards accepted. For details:
Telephone: 01624 677237
Fax: 01624 670923
Email: bookshop@enterprise.net
www.bookpost.co.uk

Free postage and packing in the United Kingdom